SCAREDY KATE

Jacob Grant

BARRON'S

For Jamie, the bravest person I know.

Text and illustrations copyright
© 2014 Jacob Grant

All inquiries should be addressed to:
Barron's Educational Series, Inc.
250 Wireless Boulevard
Hauppauge, New York 11788
www.barronseduc.com

ISBN: 978-1-4380-0364-1

Library of Congress Control No.: 2013950185

Date of Manufacture: January 2015
Manufactured by: V05I05N, Shenzhen, China

Printed in China

9 8 7 6 5 4 3

The beast stares at Kate with cold eyes.

Her aunt calls it Cookie.

Kate calls it a MONSTER.

Suddenly the monster springs from the couch!

"Aaah!"

Kate sighs with relief.
The hall is calm and quiet.

"Oh, what's that?"

"Someone must've lost this funny box."

With a "Shoomp!" the doors slide shut and the
elevator begins to rise.

"Uh-oh."

It stops at the 2nd floor...

...and a monster with
2 giant ears waddles on!

Next, the elevator stops at the 3rd floor...

...and on hops a creature
with 3 buggy eyes!

Then at the 4th floor...

...the biggest beast yet floats
on with **4** flapping wings!

And on the 5th floor, a thing with
5 feathers struts aboard!

6th floor, **6** legs!

7th floor, **7** horns!

8th floor, **8** whiskers!

9th floor, **9**... stickers?

But at the 10th floor...

Remembering the box, Kate summons all of her courage.

"DELIV

ERY!"

She opens her eyes to find that the monsters

have gathered for... ICE CREAM?

And thanks to Kate, sprinkles!

Not many people know that monsters like ice cream. But they do.

Especially with sprinkles.

Which gives Kate an idea.

"Yup, this monster likes ice cream, too."